D1179166

LIBRARIES NI
WITHDRAWN FROM STOCK

Hippo's Birthday

by Jill Atkins and Steve Cox

W
FRANKLIN WATTS
LONDON•SYDNEY

Hippo lived in a red house

by the park.

Zebra and Elephant

lived by the park, too.

So did Monkey and Giraffe.

It was Hippo's birthday.

Everyone went to her house.

Hippo was making

a birthday cake.

"Giraffe, will you help me?"
said Hippo.

"Sorry," said Giraffe. "I must go."

5

"Zebra, will you help me
with my cake?" said Hippo.
"You can help me mix it."

"Sorry," said Zebra.

"I must go, too."

"Will you help me, Elephant?"
said Hippo.
"I am making a cake."

"No," said Elephant.

"I can't help you."

"Will you help me, Monkey?"
said Hippo.

"Will you help me with my cake?"

"Sorry, I am busy, too,"
said Monkey.

Hippo was sad.

"I will have to make

my birthday cake," she said.

She looked on the shelf.

"Oh no," said Hippo.

"I need butter, eggs, sugar

and some flour."

She went to the shop.

On the way she met Giraffe,

Zebra, Elephant and Monkey.

"See you soon!" they said.

Hippo went home.

She saw a letter on the mat.

The letter said,

"Come to the park at 2 o'clock."

Hippo went to the park.

"Happy Birthday!" said Giraffe,

Zebra, Elephant and Monkey.

"We made a cake for you!"

they said.

19

Story trail

Start

Start at the beginning of the story trail. Ask your child to retell the story in their own words, pointing to each picture in turn to recall the sequence of events.

Independent Reading

This series is designed to provide an opportunity for your child to read on their own. These notes are written for you to help your child choose a book and to read it independently.

In school, your child's teacher will often be using reading books which have been banded to support the process of learning to read. Use the book band colour your child is reading in school to help you make a good choice. *Hippo's Birthday* is a good choice for children reading at Green Band in their classroom to read independently.

The aim of independent reading is to read this book with ease, so that your child enjoys the story and relates it to their own experiences.

About the book

It is Hippo's birthday and she wants to bake a birthday cake. But her friends pretend they are all too busy to help. They have planned a surprise ... and baked a birthday cake for her.

Before reading

Help your child to learn how to make good choices by asking:
"Why did you choose this book? Why do you think you will enjoy it?"
Look at the cover together and ask: "What do you think the story will be about?" Support your child to think of what they already know about the story context. Read the title aloud and ask: "What do you think Hippo is doing on the cover of the book?"
Remind your child that they can try to sound out the letters to make a word if they get stuck.
Decide together whether your child will read the story independently or read it aloud to you.

During reading

If reading aloud, support your child if they hesitate or ask for help by telling the word. Remind your child of what they know and what they can do independently.

If reading to themselves, remind your child that they can come and ask for your help if stuck.

After reading

Support comprehension by asking your child to tell you about the story. Use the story trail to encourage your child to retell the story in the right sequence, in their own words.

Help your child think about the messages in the book that go beyond the story and ask: "Do you think Hippo enjoyed her birthday in the end? Why/why not?"

Give your child a chance to respond to the story: "Did you have a favourite part? Do you have a birthday cake when it is your birthday?"

Extending learning

Help your child understand the story structure by using the same story context and adding different elements. "Let's make up a new story about one of Hippo's friends having a surprise party. Which animal will you choose? What might this animal like to eat at their party? Where would they like to have a party?"

In the classroom, your child's teacher may be teaching polysyllabic words (words with more than one syllable). There are many in this book that you could look at with your child:

Hipp/o, Mon/key, Gi/raffe, Zeb/ra, El/e/phant, birth/day.

Franklin Watts
First published in Great Britain in 2017
by The Watts Publishing Group

Copyright © The Watts Publishing Group 2017

All rights reserved.

Series Editors: Jackie Hamley and Melanie Palmer
Series Advisors: Dr Sue Bodman and Glen Franklin
Series Designer: Peter Scoulding

A CIP catalogue record for this book is
available from the British Library.

ISBN 978 1 4451 5441 1 (hbk)
ISBN 978 1 4451 5442 8 (pbk)
ISBN 978 1 4451 6092 4 (library ebook)

Printed in China

Franklin Watts
An imprint of
Hachette Children's Group
Part of The Watts Publishing Group
Carmelite House
50 Victoria Embankment
London EC4Y 0DZ

An Hachette UK Company
www.hachette.co.uk

www.franklinwatts.co.uk

FSC
www.fsc.org
MIX
Paper from
responsible sources
FSC® C104740